KUESSIPAN

KUESSIPAN

Naomi Fontaine

translated by David Homel

Arsenal Pulp Press   Vancouver

KUESSIPAN
by Naomi Fontaine
English translation copyright © 2013 by David Homel

SECOND PRINTING: 2022

Originally published in French as Kuessipan, © Mémoire d'encrier, 2011

ARSENAL PULP PRESS
Suite 202 – 211 East Georgia St.
Vancouver, BC V6A 1Z6
Canada
arsenalpulp.com

The publisher gratefully acknowledges the support of the Canada Council for the Arts and the British Columbia Arts Council for its publishing program, and the Government of Canada (through the Canada Book Fund) and the Government of British Columbia (through the Book Publishing Tax Credit Program) for its publishing activities.

Cover photographs by Isabelle Alexandra Ricq
Editing by Susan Safyan
Book design by Gerilee McBride

Printed and bound in Canada

Library and Archives Canada Cataloguing in Publication

Fontaine, Naomi, 1987–
[Kuessipan. English]
    Kuessipan / Naomi Fontaine ; translated by David Homel.

Originally published in French.
Issued in print and electronic formats.
ISBN 978-1-55152-517-4 (pbk.).—ISBN 978-1-55152-518-1 (epub)

    I. Homel, David, translator II. Title. III. Title: Kuessipan. English

PS8611.O5712K8313 2013   C843'.6   C2013-903296-7
                                                 C2013-903297-5

to my mother who figured it out
to Lucille for her friendship
to Marcorel, my poem

Kuessipan, in the Innu language,
means "your move" or "your turn"

NOMAD

I've invented lives. The man with the drum never told me about himself. I wove a story from his gnarled hands and his bent back. He mumbled to himself in an ancient, distant language. I acted like I knew all about him. The man I invented—I loved him. And the other lives I embellished. I wanted to see the beauty; I wanted to create it. Change the nature of things—I don't want to name them—so that I see only the embers that still burn in the hearts of the first inhabitants. Pride is a symbol; pain is the price I don't want to pay. Still, I invented, I built a false world, a reconstructed reserve where kids play outside and women have children to love them and the language survives. I wish things had been easier to say and tell and write down on the page, without expecting anything except to be understood. But who wants to read words like drugs, incest, alcohol, loneliness, suicide, bad cheque, rape? I hurt, and I haven't even spoken yet. I haven't talked about anybody. I don't dare yet.

Dense fog. The poor visibility makes the drivers slow down. Sometimes they put on their flashers to help each other get oriented. The road is wet. No one takes a chance on passing. In the dark, you see better with the headlights on low. It won't last more than a few minutes, an hour.

He says, Fog in the morning means a sunny day. Fog in the evening, a rainy morning tomorrow.

They blamed the fog. It was the usual mist you get on May evenings. The damp wind off the sea carries grey clouds over the road from Uashat to Mani-utenam. The fog must have been thick, opaque, and impenetrable. It must have been a black night, dark and moonless. The other cars shouldn't have been there. He should have been the only one on the road, finding his way, moving through the humid air. Trees and poles should have gone and hidden in the thick grey cover. Fear, inexperience, speed, recklessness, taking chances—a way out.

I'm always afraid to drive in the fog.

I wish you could meet the girl with the round belly. The one who will raise her children on her own. Who will scream at her man when he cheats on her. Who will cry all alone in the living room, who will change diapers all her life. Who will look for work at thirty, finish high school at thirty-five, who will start living too late, who will die too soon, completely exhausted and unsatisfied.

Of course I lied. I threw a white veil over the dirt.

A car wreck. The fear of losing my child. The insults used against the Innu. Death. Missing fathers. Clear-cutting up north. My cousin's poor life with her two children, and my inability to help her. The abused children. My mother's criticism. Gabriel, when he doesn't call back. The movies that are too beautiful to be true. Oppression. Injustice. Cruelty. Loneliness. Love songs. Unforgiveable mistakes. The babies who will never be born.

◂▴▸

Or this: the grey skin of a man who is too young for the varnished wooden box with its gilt patterns and golden handles. His eyes sleep, and his fine lips express nothing: a lifeless face. The flowers on the box surround the prayer etched on a piece of wood: *I am never far…*

I hate the faces of the dead, their serene features and closed eyes. The absurdity of cold skin blotched with sad colours, like November when the sky is grey. I hate the wrinkles they will never have, the souls departed, taking with them all existence in a single breath. I hate looking at them. The custom says we must sit with them. I am dying of their ugliness, these men with lifeless eyes.

Why won't his eyes ever reflect my face? I want his mouth, forever mute, to tell me that I look like him.

◄▲►

When we were girls, we played together over summer vacation. You were slimmer, paler, shyer than me. You wore a red T-shirt that was too big for you, and I wore a white top over a yellow T-shirt. It was a time of carefree secrets and childish seduction. We were too silly to believe in love. You used to sleep over, like a sister.

The summers slipped away, one after the other. One evening you showed up in tears. I remember. You explained it, but we didn't understand. I cried without knowing why. We fell asleep together in dreamless slumber that made our eyes go puffy. Your mother had started drinking again.

The next day, they placed you with one of our aunts. An emergency measure. You laughed that day. Nothing showed from the outside. In my head, I prayed to Jesus, very fast, without you noticing.

I know the world is unfair.

◂▲▸

Why does it have to be this way? At night, her sleep is so heavy it pushes her forehead into the dune of her pillow. Her face trembles in the darkness of a closed room. She stiffens whenever anyone raises his voice. Fear pursues her into her nightmares of motherhood. She cries, and no one comforts her. She forgets, then laughs.

I want to tell her that I know. And why I say nothing.

That silence. I'd like to write that silence.

◄▲►

A child is following him, watching him intently because of his good looks and the silver rings he wears on his fingers—or so he thinks. He smiles at the child and asks him who his father is. I don't have one, the child answers.

He's sorry he asked. He should have asked who his mother is.

Everyone knows he dyes his grey hair. He slips cheap rings onto his fingers and puts on his fringed leather jacket to take a drive around the reserve. It gives him an excuse to keep his speed down. He has the darkened complexion of a man who has abused alcohol, worked in the sun, and grown old. Cheeks, forehead, hands—all wrinkled. I've done it all in this life. The oratory of the sewing machine operator, the choker-man, the fisherman, the hunter, the gas-jockey, the lineman, the lumberman, the carpenter. The bum on the street, he adds. His laughter is broken by smoke. When he talks that way, he uses French, but the language doesn't quite make it out of his throat and gives the lie to his self-assurance.

He currently lives with one of his sisters. He has the biggest room in the basement. His furnishings can be quickly enumerated: a box of DVDs, a shelf lined with perfume bottles, a full-length mirror, a flannel bathrobe, cowboy boots set aside for another day, a bed perfectly centred against the wall, always carefully made.

This morning, he left without his aging adolescent get-up. He's working as a wildlife officer for the Band Council. In his cabin on the Moisie River, he notes down the catches and checks the fishermen who aren't Innu. Three months' work for nine months' unemployment. After a few days, he'll go back to his sister's for a shower. Then he'll set out again, his body and mind finally a man's.

◂▴▸

These are letters to my baby. To my mother. To my big sister.
To God. To my father. To Lucille. To Jean-Yves. To the education officer of the Uashat and Mani-utenam Band Council. To
my ex's parents. To my ex. To myself. To my little sister. To the
Premier of Quebec. To my brother. To Gabriel. To my older
cousin Luc. To Nicolas D. To William—not the prince. To
the cruel world. To my tribe. To M's father. To the sad people.
To the children of the future.

◄▲►

The roads never look the same: the one that heads north, and the other that brings us back again. Rough, dusty tracks made of loose dirt, potholes, and curves, which we drive on carefully. Asphalt roads with lines painted on them: they take us exactly where we want to go, no detours, but with slow-downs at rush hour. Isolated roads that dream of being driven on, others that let themselves go, since no one ever takes them.

The road he followed, from the beginning of autumn to the first snow, took him to his cabin with no stops along the way, except maybe for a porcupine he came across. Then he would stop and go after it. Three hours of chaos to reach the intimacy of a lake much too beautiful to remain hidden, but too remote for most human eyes. His land was there. He was too old for the hunt now, too young to let the land go. He occupied it the way you occupy part of a room, in silence, but with the contentment of being on your own territory. He felt at home. Close to nature, close to the infinities the sky offered on full-moon nights, intimate with creative strength. He was old, but his body was still vigorous enough for confrontation and survival. He stood straight, though his bark had stiffened and wrinkled. He built the first cabin and made others spring from the earth. He stood straight, demanding of the land what it had always given him. Master of his roots, he was humble before the beauty of a cloudless October evening. The twilight was golden. He was grateful to see his grandchildren playing with branches and sand. He was the promise of what we must never desert—a dusty, rutted road, especially in autumn, especially for us.

Nomad: I like to imagine this is a natural way of living.

UASHAT

He says, A sad song is something from the heart, like the blues. The Innu language is like music that you sing, with slow intonations that you stretch out further with your breath. There are no vowels, and that makes the language impenetrable, like a return to nature: harsh, all bark and antlers.

Neka, my mother. *Mashkuss*, bear cub. *Nikuss*, my son.
Mikun, feather. *Anushkan*, raspberry. *Auetiss*, baby beaver.
Ishkuess, girl. *Nitanish*, my daughter. *Tshiuetin*, the north
wind. *Mishtapeu*, a big man. *Menutan*, a rain shower.
Shukapesh, the man who is robust. *Kanataushiht*, the hunters.
Pishu, lynx. *Kakuss*, young porcupine. *Kupaniesh*, a man who
is an employee. *Tshishteshinu*, our big brother. *Tshukuminu*,
our grandmother. *Nuta*, my father.

The gatherings go on late, lasting long after the sun goes
down. The screech of the radio brings out the men. The
snowmobile lights up just enough of the path to keep from
getting bogged down. It growls in the silence of hibernating
bears. Tonight, neither the city nor the airplanes colour the
sky with a soft purple as sinuous as a wolf. The little girl's eyes
say thank you for having seen it.

◄▲►

The house is green. The sirens that beat against the glass panel of the door are red and blue. The glass is covered in condensation from the warm air inside and the cold outside. The dogs howl endlessly after a distant wolf. They call out for confrontation like their owners in the house. They howl at the sirens to stop. They're not afraid of anything.

The girls are scared when they're on their own at night. The doors are locked and the windows shut tight, even in summer. The fences don't keep anyone out. The howling comes from outside.

The only ones frightened by the endlessly turning red and blue sirens are the girls, quiet within their walls, watching, sheltered by darkness.

It's happening a few meters away. The sirens have stopped. The sirens don't scare anyone now.

Night is when you get undressed.

The top and the bottom of your body are bare. Your cheeks are red. Your tears are warm. You have dreams and say nothing about them in order not to be afraid. You lie down upon the sand. The filth. The others have been there before you. Drunkenness. Red eyes. Forgetfulness. In the night, you see only what your hands can touch.

A shadow—the reflection of a human being. That shadow is you. Thin hollow cheeks, averted eyes that won't focus and don't want to be seen. Tired, weak shoulders and ashen skin, two teeth missing. A smile that's too timid to turn to laughter, afraid of what others might say. I picture your eyes, their shape and dark colour, and see the paradox of beauty and suffering.

In the big cities, it's easier to be nobody. The people on the street know nothing about you. They glance at you, no more, then think of something else. A few months back, you left the reserve and the village that knows you, your family and friends, and went to live like a stranger in the emptiness of the city. Your apartment belongs to you alone, along with the used furniture you bought for next to nothing. You have a round wooden table that sits in one corner of the kitchen and two empty chairs. A sofa covered in blue velvet. The fridge rumbles and freezes your food instead of keeping it cold. The bedroom window looks out on the storefront of the building next door. At night, you hear the cars going by on the expressway. It's different than where you're from.

Back home, in winter, the wind is dry and icy. The sea and the river call for the ocean. Your house was built in a bay, a sandy bay covered in snow six months a year. There are woods nearby, some pine and spruce, a beach facing the islands. There are children everywhere, which explains the laughter and tears. The houses are all rectangular, with sand in front, wooden fences, and doors you practically never lock except at night or when you're away. People don't knock before they walk in; they're used to the warmth of the fire and the ease of a canvas tent. Only a stranger would knock, but there aren't very many of those. They don't venture onto the reserve.

One summer, you left on a group project that the Band Council put together with young people to try and stop the violence. You pitched your tents on the beach on one of the islands, the biggest of the seven sheltered by the bay. Forest covered this piece of earth sculpted by salt water. Isolated, gazing upon infinity, the world took on all its meaning. You felt the instinct of the old hunters, ready to face the land in times of starvation. You wanted to stay forever on that island, do battle with it, become a warrior, a hero. Like in the movie with that actor whose name you never knew—a lone survivor, alone and lost, and surviving somehow. But at dawn, it was time to leave.

When you were little, you spent all day outside, playing with your brother, building cabins, making mud pies with wet sand, and watching the neighbours drive off in their cars, then come back a few hours later. A piece of toast with peanut butter, a slice of cheese, and fruit juice for breakfast. Time was meaningless, like a truck forgotten in a parking lot, like a dandelion you thought was a rose —a child's existence. Sometimes there was nothing for lunch. You climbed onto a chair, took down the biggest bowl you could reach, and served yourself a generous helping of brightly coloured cereal. It tasted good. Then you went back to your friends, who were there where you'd left them by the schoolyard. There weren't as many as before. They were all waiting for the bell, even the ones who hadn't gone back to their houses.

At first, you were too young for the parties that went on forever. No more than twelve the first time you blacked out: a silly smile and your cap on backwards. Your eyes had narrowed down to two dots. There was no pain there. No more, any more. Then it came into your life, the thing that seemed too small to be deadly. Get your hands on it, crush it, inhale it. Then be strong. It was all over the reserve, in the houses, on the street. They sold it in small doses, one pill at a time, almost cheap. It was a drug for the poor. The nights went on for weeks. There were no limits. There never had been.

One night, you felt an unspeakable pain between your ribs, then in your guts, like a metal bar piercing your body. You went to the hospital for tests. They found the problem quickly enough: it was your liver. Completely destroyed. You had abused it and it became intolerant. You had to stop using immediately, right now. You were twenty years old.

You went to the city for treatment. You left your village, your poverty, your self-destruction, your friends and family. You started anew somewhere else, and gave it your best shot. You took care of yourself to survive. You were a survivor of your own body. You had to do it. At the end of that filthy journey, you still had hope. So you left.

Like all the other boys, you dreamed of being a fireman, building a house, falling in love. You were little, sitting on the bottom step of the stairs, and you spotted a new car moving slowly up the street. You were going to drive the same kind later on. It would be black, a luxury model, with a girl too pretty for you at your side. You were going to be someone important, a band councillor or a rich worker. You didn't dream of being the best. You just wanted to be among the better ones.

Did anyone ever tell you that you're beautiful?

From a distance, it looks like Paris, with the lit-up factory reaching toward the sky like that famous tower. But who here has ever seen Paris? The sand is soft and the air warm. People look into the fire, and their faces glow. They're not allowed here. Who says? The whites who tried to expropriate the bay to build roads and bridges and houses at $1,000 a square foot. But the bay is just fine the way it is, and the people are sufficient unto themselves, with their faces illuminated by the flames of the forbidden. Of course, their eyes are shining. The anticipation of staying up late, losing consciousness, losing their pain and hatred. The many hatreds that feed them. From a distance, they are only shadows, then little by little their human shapes emerge. You hear a guitar, the laughter of a drunk girl, rustling clothing, people listening eagerly, stories that smear mud on the neighbours, and everyone knows who. Another night on the smooth sand of the bay.

On the beach, when you look eastward, you can't even see the far shore. That's why the children say they're swimming in the sea and because of the water, too, which tastes salty, and the waves. The houses stand together tightly, imitating each other. This tiny village they call a reserve. The streets: Pashin. De Queen. Grégoire. Arnaud. Kamin. Sand comes up to the front of the houses and covers the asphalt and the welcome mats. Behind the Galeries Montagnaises, nothing but sand. The car starts up. Say whatever you like, I'm still leaving home.

Galix. Port-Cartier. Baie-Trinité. Baie-Comeau. Forestville. Places I'd hate to live in.

There's nowhere worth stopping, but a tank of gas won't get you there. At Les Escoumins, there's a gas station where, upon presentation of a card, you don't have to pay tax. If you're not Indian, there's no sense going there.

That's the grade school that they built a few years ago. When you look at it from above, you see it's shaped like a bird. An eagle, I think. Trying to be poetic. My mother works in the school. She helps students with problems, with attention deficits, in special classes. She teaches one of her nephews. One day, she gave him ten dollars because she wanted to make him happy. That same day, one of her students asked her if he could have ten dollars too. It's funny, you see. She said it was an experiment, like a science project. It's not like she's young; she started studying later in life. She had us, then we grew up, and she wanted something more. I admire her, that's for sure, the way all girls admire their mothers, I guess.

That's the daycare. The project took a while to get off the ground. The place looks like a doghouse painted orange; I like blue better, and the bird shape. Incoherent, dreamy girls: the one coming to get her daughter is my cousin on my father's side. She's twenty-two, but she looks five years younger; she's tiny and very pretty. She started back at school this year. Her eldest daughter is in kindergarten. Her boyfriend is studying in Forestville. That's four hours from here, on the way to Quebec City. They must not see each other very often. I remember when I lived there, and I was separated from my sweetheart. I was sad most of the time, like a dog that's stopped wagging its tail.

If you keep going, you'll come to the Catholic cemetery. There aren't many graves, and it's not because people aren't dying. The first cemetery is on the other side of the reserve. The people who died after the 1960s are all buried here, like my grandfather Alexandre on my mother's side. In Innu, we say *Anikashan*, so that's how they got the name. He's got a nice stone monument for himself and my grandmother. When I was little, it sat in the yard behind his house. We would run circles around it and hang off the arms that stuck out. We didn't know that one day it would stand for someone's memory, and that the fun of swinging from it would disappear. I never really knew my grandfather. We didn't understand what he said, since his teeth had all fallen out. When he asked us for something, like a glass of water, we couldn't even help out. Then he would get up, and we would all scatter. I was young, but I knew he was someone admirable. I would see the elders wave to him from their porches. The young artists would stop at his house to visit. People would watch him work — not to listen to him muttering, but to see what his worn hands had to teach them. As I grew up, I understood he wasn't like other old people desperately trying to teach us what they knew. He gave — that's all. Without forcing future craftsmen to follow his way. An elder. He lived in his house till the day he died. I'd like to tell you that it's always that way among the Innu. That, in Uashat, there's no such thing as an old folks' home, a hidden place where their pain is invisible. But you'd know I was lying when you saw the new building on Arnaud Street that they call the Long-Term Care. The old folks won't go there. They keep expecting that one of their granddaughters will come and make bread, and that their great-grandson will drive them to church on Sunday. They'll have the last word, I suppose. My great-grandmother lived to 101, and till her very last day, her relatives streamed in and out of her house. She was tiny and fragile and diminished by many winters, but she ran her domain with a firm hand, faithful to her woman's customs. At her funeral, the church was filled to overflowing, and people spilled onto the square outside. My cousin read a poem. My aunt named all her descendants. I was sitting with my mother and my sisters, in silence. I didn't know anything about this woman named Blandine whom people called *Mishta-An-Auass*, but I was proud to be part of her legacy. I didn't cry. I almost never cry.

The ball field has always been there. The red paint is washed out, and the white is peeling. They have softball tournaments in the summer. People from the village meet there. Kids climb on the grandstands. Young mothers come to watch their boyfriends hit the ball. They glance over at their kids playing in the sand. When the heat turns humid, the fans don't stay long; they get up as soon as the game is over. Other people take their spots. At night, teenagers hang out there. They meet on the bottom step of the grandstands. They laugh hard and talk loud, pointing their fingers and waving their arms. That's because they're drunk, and they forget to be shy. It's time for excess, all night long, until their madness reaches the first bluish light of dawn.

You can't get lost on the reserve, so don't worry, even though this girl's so little. Even three-year-old kids can play without anyone watching them. The drivers are used to it; they go slowly. People walk slowly too. That girl who's coming our way, the fat one in the black sweater, she's a distant cousin. Our parents are cousins. She has three kids. I think she's pregnant again. They say she's talking about getting an abortion, but I don't think it's true. Girls don't get abortions here. They endure, they survive. Sometimes they enjoy the ephemeral pleasures of alcohol. Most of the time, they can't find anyone to look after their children; they're too young and there are too many of them. They accept it. That's how they save their souls, I suppose. My cousin always laughs loud with one hand over her mouth. Typical. If she was slimmer, she'd be pretty. Her hair flows down to the middle of her back when she doesn't put it up. She has the eyes of an Indian woman who's seen it all and is amazed she can still laugh. A look that burns from the inside of existence. See, now she's beautiful.

If you keep going straight, pretty soon you'll have sand beneath your feet. You'll taste the salty air. The sun will start to go down. The sky will put on a show. Let the waves rock your senses. You will be comforted. Walk through those spruce trees and you'll see the bay, the beach with its soft sand, the aluminum smelter, the islands, the river as wide as the sea. The ocean, from which you came.

◄▲►

Not many people are out walking during the day, just some women with their strollers. A fifteen-year-old girl is dragging her round belly from a blue house to a beige one. She has circles under her eyes. A long night spent waiting for her boyfriend. The date the welfare cheque arrives will determine whether he'll show up. A pickup truck moves slowly up Pashin Street. Doors stay open all day long from June to September. At night, kids run in packs. Cases of twenty-four. Shouting late at night, fighting early in the morning. The doors are locked now. In winter, snowmobile tracks run down both sides of the street. When the wind is icy, no one goes out walking; car engines never stop running. At the end of Kamin Street, there's a little girl with almond eyes. Raspberries grow behind her house in blue springtime when the asphalt dries. This is the centre of her world.

The river water is sweet. It will quench your thirst and revive you after the long autumn portage. The women are strong; they carry their youngest on their backs. Sweat on their brows, shoulders tired, their eyes fixed on the ground. Silence rules. You tire less if you don't talk. The three families follow along the riverbank. They will walk another four days. They'll camp where the river narrows.

The old man talks about the weather. He's worried about a dry winter. He goes quiet, hoping he'll be wrong. The eldest of the women finishes cooking the bread in the ashes. Caribou fat gives them the strength to continue the journey. The little girl runs to the river and bends over until her chin touches the water. With her two tiny hands, she gathers a sweet swallow. Then repeats, again and again. Finally, her thirst from the long journey is quenched. Satisfied, she picks up the little cloth bag and slings it over her back. It contains the essentials.

In a circle around the fire, the guests await the bride. They hold hands and their palms are moist. The girl in the purple dress is sitting by the man in a suit and tie and a woman she doesn't know, who is holding a sleeping child in her arms. The sun gently burns the cheeks of the two nations united this afternoon to witness the marriage between an Innu man and a white woman.

The master of the traditional ceremony explains his dream in *atikamek*, then translates it into French, a very second language. The betrothed and his sweetheart offer their witnesses pieces of sculpted wood. The witnesses promise their support. Some cry. The circle tightens.

Now they bind their hands with scarves and string. No one hears the "I do" that their hearts speak. You can see the promise in their eyes as they stand in the centre of the world, as she cries and smiles at the same time.

There's no paper to sign, no vows to repeat, no monologues. They have chosen to love one another like savages with a pure love, without legal constraint. A love that will last. The lovers promise that to each of their guests: In turn, they receive a nod of their heads, a kind of gratitude.

The girl in the purple dress presses her body against her sweetheart in his Sunday best. She loves him.

◀▲▶

The women are the first to respond to the beat of the drum. They rise to their feet, one after the other, dancing with one foot forward, the back one slightly bent, as if they were limping. Their chant deepens their movements, each slow step, their hands close to their bodies, smiles on their faces. Intuition tightens the circle. One woman, who is more daring than the others, lets loose with a cry, an Indian woman's cry, strong and high-pitched. Laughter breaks out as the others echo her voice. The movements grow stronger, some roll their shoulders, they quicken the beat of their hands against their hips. The younger ones follow, imitating their parents. The circle widens and the chairs empty. Then the drum slows and with it, the dance. They applaud the old man and his song, which comes from the past. Eyes meet and faces are proud: the desire to be yourself.

Somewhere before Tadoussac, caught between two mountains, is a lake that reflects the things of this Earth. On the bank, a dock and some canoes. A wooden cabin sending smoke into the air. No one swims in the lake. When the leaves redden, the lake bursts into the colour of flames. It burns. When the snow covers it completely, the canoes disappear. Then the lake stops reflecting the jewel of blue heaven. Nothing but its pale skin and the thousands of grey spruce remain to speak of its beauty.

Even from a distance, you can see the lights. Of course it's impossible to make out the bridge and the highways, the traffic lights and the lampposts. The lights of the Château Frontenac and the ones on top of Complex G. The house lights are scarcely visible, but they are part of the orange halo that forms in the sky. This is what the city has done.

It's salmon season. On the *Mishta-Shipu*, the canoes follow
the rhythm of the big catches and the smaller ones. The air
is cool, and the sun shines. A few flies wander across the skin
of the Innu who have taken back possession of this place.
On the riverbank they have pitched their tents: beige canvas
covers the wooden poles bound to one another by yellow
rope. The women have covered the ground with freshly cut
pine branches. The fishermen rarely sleep in these shelters.
The families fill them. The ones who have too many children
have no idea how to occupy their offspring. Some men have
chosen not to touch strong drink during the warmest period.
Here, the land is sacred. The men don't come here to drink,
and neither do the young people. Silence does a world of
good for those who listen to it; sometimes you can hear a
salmon swimming upstream.

These people go any way they want to—in front of the houses, behind them, alongside, if they feel like it. Every year, the Council hires seasonal workers to build fences around the new houses. People who are used to taking shortcuts keep going their usual way. The woman who lives in the beige and brown house at the corner of Kamin and Pashin comes out and yells at the man on her property to stop climbing over her fence. He pays her no attention. He's just passing through and wants to meet his friend who's waiting for him. He could always knock down a few planks to make his way easier. Then she'd have something to yell about. The woman never yells at the drunkards. That's because she buys her beer at the same store they do, right behind her house. No sense asking the owner to put up a high barrier to keep all those lazy guys from breaking down the old fence that she keeps having to repair.

There, at the beginning. A fence, higher than a man. The metal surrounds the wooden cabins battered by the constant wind blowing off the sea, cabins scattered and sunk into the earth. The town stops where the reserve begins. The fence was put up to keep out wolves and Innu. They both lurk behind the barrier, waiting close by. They're looking for a way through, to the path of their own laws. They want to escape to a place without barricades.

They built the Baptist church in front of the reserve's Catholic cemetery. The pastor had been talking about it for a while. They built it over the summer and painted it green and white. People were talking; you could hear words of discontent and anger. The most radical swore they'd burn it down. Others weren't looking for a fight, but they weren't looking for Baptists either.

The Jesuits taught Catholicism to the Innu, and that faith lives on in the Innu soul. The Catholic religion was learned, acquired. It is practically a tradition, with priests present in the memory of the nation. People have forgotten just one thing: how the Innu were "emancipated" by being sent to the residential schools. How the Indians, who never wanted to be white, were kidnapped, the children scattered, taken elsewhere during the hard months of the school year to give, so they were told, some meaning to their intelligence. This family feud will never be settled; how can the son ask the father for forgiveness? A cinder on the heart, one more wrinkle on the brow.

A dozen cars are parked in front of the house. People are smoking on the porch or inside. Some of them are weary of blowing smoke out of their nostrils or mouths; those are the ones who have been smoking the longest. They wait. They watch. They have taken over the deceased's house. Out of sympathy, out of respect, knowledge, feeling, pain, reason, kinship, friendship, sharing, gratitude—out of authority.

The florist sets up first in the living room. Roses, tulips, carnations—everything is the colour of summer. People stare at the bouquets.

The hearse is black and lustrous. Men dressed in suits and ties pull the coffin from the car. Solemnly, they move up the front steps. People gather around, leaving enough space for the men, then press together when they have placed the coffin against the widest wall of the living room. The florist returns and scatters more bouquets at the front, sides, and on top of the casket. A few cigarettes are still burning in the ashtrays. A song flows from the heart of an old woman; she launches into the first couplet.

The dead man's wake lasts three days and three nights. A dozen chairs have been set out in front of the coffin, for prayers and contemplation. Coffee and tea are abundant. The visitors bring meat loaf, pies, fruit, and sandwiches.

I can't bring myself to kiss the dead man, or even approach him, or kiss his hands in a sign of love and devotion. I don't want to look at him—I can't. I pay my respects from the farthest chair. I'm afraid if I cry, I'll be misunderstood. I keep the silence and contemplate his face with a single glance, not comprehending death. I think of his grandfather, his grandmother, his father. I manage to embrace the dead man's family, and leave.

Now he is in the ground. The house is empty. One car is parked in front. The silence echoes the prayers murmured the evening before. The floor dirtied by many pairs of shoes. The TV is turned off, sitting in the spot where the casket had been, where the eldest had opened it, without flinching, as if used to seeing corpses. The photo of the young man, whose strength and greatness were praised so highly this morning at the final tribute, is framed and set on a small wooden table in the corner of the living room, his face mute and care-worn for all eternity.

A tall table for meals, and an armchair where my baby sleeps.
My sister and my mother snoring away. Blankets are set out on
the floor. A door slams.

A bed as big as the world. Melted chocolate in a coffee pot.
A few half-finished beers sit on the table. You can see your
body from head to toe in the tall mirror. The window looks
out onto hundreds of lights. There are oils that smell like
watermelon. Soft light, the way you like it.

A sloping ceiling, like a chalet. The walls are violet and
turquoise. The blankets are warm in the unheated room, the
sheets rumpled from the effort of nights together. A night can
hold so much. A burst of laughter, then sighs. The morning
hours that add up. The scent of something hard to name, then
it fades. Fake flowers with fake petals. The room is too small.

The black ants can't wait to climb up the pickers' anklcs.
Blueberries grow where the forest left its ashes.

Squatting, her back bent, she drags her half-filled bucket
from bush to bush.

The forest burned. On a white plastic sign, in red letters:
No trespassing. A little further on: Site of future blueberry
farm.

◀▲▶

The house is small and perched on sand. There's no one to decorate the lot. It has a wooden fence around it. Its blue walls are dull, nearly grey, and tired. The house is the only one of its kind, with this design. The sand swallows up the garbage and the few empty beer bottles that no one has bothered to pick up. Against the walls, meagre weeds grow, scattered along the front of the house, three metres long from one end to the other. The wooden porch is overgrown with dogs and softened by rain. The cement footings stick out two feet. The metal chair is for summer and can be folded away at night. The windows have never been redone, and cold morning drafts of dry December air blow in. Fingerprints smudge the kitchen windows. A smell of mold rises from in front of the beige door. Something is decomposing and looking to do harm, stretching its ill will all the way to the house next door.

There's the primary and the secondary school, the Band Council, and the Catholic church. There are hundreds of houses, but only three designs. The park has been vandalized. Garbage is heaped at the street corners, along the fences, by the houses. Some houses are under construction; others are being demolished. The cemetery has wooden crosses with flowers at their feet and stone statues. The daycare has been painted orange. The field is overrun with vermin; the open square exposed to the elements, where the sun sets and the winds howl. The rink is used as a basketball court in the summer. There is a park with grandstands. The heated pool is fenced off, full of kids wearing bathing caps. The smell of the sea is nearby, and the sand slopes down to the bay. The water is polluted by the aluminum smelter. There's Grande-Basque Island, then the ocean.

The men did the work, all of them volunteers. They chose a vacant lot in front of the clinic. They agreed to start building on a Saturday. The Council supplied the materials. They built a community hall for weddings, funerals, holidays, and Innu concerts. The work lasted four full days. The less observant skipped Mass. There was no foundation, just a rectangular frame and siding and a wooden gable. They had a community supper for the inauguration with caribou, partridge, meat pies, hare. Full to the brim, they danced and laughed until the wee hours of the morning.

Some years later, it only took a few hours to demolish the place.

To Saint Mary: behind the whiteness of her skin, she is red from head to toe. Red, the colour of embers rising from a fire, the colour of a sunset during summer heat, the colour of blood that flows from the fur of the animals of the hunt. She strains, pushed forward by a burden too heavy for her shoulders. In a language not her own, she tries to describe the world she lived in, untangle the low notes of those who have been drawn upward, and she will grow thinner with each chord of a scratchy guitar. She is breathing harder, she says *mamu*, and the audience understands she is talking about them and others like them, their little group of black and white heads. Alone on stage, she sings the language of a forgotten people, like a call for help, out of modesty. Her voice is clear, her soul beautiful, so as not to forget.

The fat woman, her skin burned by the sun, forever sitting on her porch—her house has been judged unfit for habitation.

She'll go and live with her daughter in Nutashkuan during the time it takes to tear it down and rebuild it.

Later, her house will fall into another family's hands.

◂▲▸

Going to her cousin's house takes her five minutes, three if she runs all the way. She pulls on her spring jacket and gym shoes and takes off to meet up with her girlfriend—no looking back. She doesn't want to be late, since her aunt is taking her to see the squirrels with her family. They'll give peanuts to the fat little rodents that are all but tame, thanks to the hikers. They'll walk for a while along the path that follows the fast-flowing river where you can't go swimming, or even dip your toes. At the end of the path is a group of doll-sized buildings: a school, a church, and a house with windows and a room upstairs. She wonders if real elves ever lived in those cottages. They must have, since who would have built such pretty little things for no reason, then let them grow old and empty?

She spots her cousin as she turns the corner. She runs even faster, and never wonders why her own mother won't take her to see the squirrels.

◀▲▶

He's tired of never being good enough. Of hearing the mother of his children yell at him. Of never having an appetite for the meals she serves him, the bland, tasteless food that the kids stuff themselves with every day. He feels stupid, sitting dully in front of the TV, watching the same old movies every afternoon. He feels stupid when he gets dressed in the morning, knowing that he'll go out only to grab a carton of milk at the store or smoke a joint with the guy next door. He even feels stupid when he's in the shower.

He wishes he could do something besides wait for a cheque on the first of every month; the money goes through his girlfriend's fingers like water before he has time to complain. But he has no idea what else he can do.

They say that men used to go hunting in the old days, for weeks at a time, and that they'd come back to their wives with enough meat to last for months. They say that when the fishing was good, there would be a big feed every night, from June till September. Even if he was away for long periods, a man was still the master of his house or his tent. They say that the men enjoyed coming back with the feeling that they'd done good work, full of strength and discipline, that masculine feeling of pride, not just because they were providers, but because they showed that they loved their families.

No one ever told him how, nowadays, he could be like one of those men.

NUTSHIMIT

Nutshimit is the back country, the land of my ancestors. Every family knows its land. The lakes are the roads up there. The rivers tell you which way north is. If you go too far, if your judgment fails you, the railroad will help you find your way.

Nutshimit is a ritual for caribou hunters. The elders can't do without that pure air. Now that they've lost the strength in their legs, they go up there just to breathe the air.

Nutshimit is land unknown, but it's not hostile for people seeking peace of mind. In the old days, men and women lived in these forests, and they took what the land offered them with their hands. They have disappeared, but on the rocks, in the falling water, the green of the spruce, they have left their imprint, their searching eyes.

For a man in a state of confusion, *Nutshimit* means peace, that inner peace he so desperately seeks. The silence after he's shouted out his pain for nights on end, without anyone hearing. The silence of the wind that sets the pine needles whispering. The silence of a partridge that struts alongside a dozen of its kind. The silence of a stream following its way, buried under a metre of snow.

The young man wants to hear what his ancestors' land has to tell him. This morning he will take the train north.

◀▲▶

They say, Go on the train. They never say, Go to the station or Go on the railroad. Going on the train is like saying you're going somewhere very far away, you're going to make that long trip to *Nutshimit* for yourself. They go on the train because it's the means of transportation they know, the only one that heads straight north along the path that the land offers it, that follows the long line of little stations until it reaches Matimekush, Lac-John, and the city of iron ore.

The building that serves as the station is old and clad in grey sheet-metal. The walls are beige. Inside it's cold in the winter because people never close the door. A few orange chairs help them wait for the hour of departure early in the morning, two times a week. The travellers stand outside, smoking and drinking sweet coffee. They're not impatient. They know they'll be leaving soon, either for one of the hundreds of cabins scattered along the rail line or for Matimekush. Families and old folks prefer the cold season for train travel. They bring their warmest coats, several packs of cigarettes, and boxes full of food, enough for the week. The men follow the season of the hunt and leave when they feel the need for time alone. They carry less: their rifles and skidoos, warm clothing, and gasoline. No meat—they trust their hunter's pride. There's no alcohol in their baggage out of respect for the land. With barely time for a hug, the babies in the women's arms, the men say *So long*, no one cries because they know that those who are leaving will find peace in the forest. No one pities them; they are envied. They smile and shake hands, their noon meals in their lunchboxes. It's eight o'clock, the start of a long road that will last hours, a day, long into the night, depending on each man's destination. The train pulls away silently, easily, to make you feel how important it is.

It's always dark when it returns. The platform is crowded, as if the hunters had been absent for months, though most of them haven't been away for more than a week. Some of them have been up north longer; they will stay up later that night. Each man has his welcome party. Many arms grab for his bags. Hugs and pats on the back, smiling faces. The essential questions are asked: how many partridges, hares, caribou did you kill? The cars drive off one by one, full of noisy passengers.

◂▴▸

Summer sends its first signals, and the child returns. He has changed. He has grown older. His mother takes this little man into her arms and cries. She doesn't recognize his voice and the way he is any more. It is a change of season. She wishes the summer would have lasted longer.

The man stands straight, his tie tightly knotted, with his black suit and ambitious smile — very straight and tall. With one hand, he brings the woman closer to his body, a small brown-skinned woman in a white dress, a smile on her tight lips. Behind them, the autumn …

Dead fur on blood-stained snow. Brought down by the rifle slung over the back of an Innu man with shining almond eyes, and the pride men show when they've killed one of the grey animals. Like a kid, his mouth is set, and his hand rests on the animal's neck. One knee on the ground, the other ready to spring. The hunter never rests.

◂▲▸

There was laughter in his head. They were talking leadership candidates, books to read, future students, kids growing up, the subjects all jumbled together. Seeing double should have been a hint; glasses of red, glasses of white. He didn't even taste it. It didn't smell like anything. Words can be important, but these meant nothing, they slipped from lips and landed on the porch next door. Blackout.

The unwilling ones revolt and confront authority. They fight to raise the flesh of their flesh, to teach them how to become men and women, a nation in their own image—not to dominate, but to subsist and live on.

The old man with the white skin put on his feathers and his colourful clothes. He slipped on his moccasins, which turned him into an Indian. With a peace pipe in his hand, he is going off to negotiate with the chief of state.

At the age of forty, she discovered her true nature. She was a mother and grandmother several times over, a woman of experience, a career woman but not a careerist. She served once as a councillor for her village. She ran for chief and lost, but wasn't a loser. Soft eyes and a familiar smile. Believing she knew enough about herself at forty, she set off with a small group to follow the path of her ancestors.

When spring comes, the nomads travel to their encampment on the road that the river makes for them. They move through mountains and valleys, rowing, walking, portaging. They are used to the work, forced to become one with nature in order to survive, taking on its forms to hold onto existence.

She wasn't ready for what came next. How could she have been? The train dropped them at Mile 150. They had supper in a cabin. The fire crackled in the woodstove, and its warmth was a comfort. The chimney smoked as much as the four women and the young man, who chatted away happily. Everyone went to sleep early. At dawn the next morning, they would have to pack their bags and leave.

It was the beginning of one thing and the end of something else. To walk, you have to put one foot in front of the other, your pack on your back, a confident smile on your lips. You go as far as the river then row, your knees on the wooden bones of a canoe that has made this journey a thousand times. You follow the river and recognize it as a path: that of the ancestors and her own people.

A few days later, she started wanting to be home again, in her house, in her bed with her man, nice and warm, clean and fresh, drinking a cup of coffee with cream and sugar in the morning. She didn't want to live like a nomad any more; she didn't want to carry everything on her back for one more second. She wasn't one of those women from the past who had no sense of time or effort, who climbed every mountain as if it were the first. How could she fight nature—starting with her own nature?

Then morning rose, as sharp as the night before. For the first time since she started out, she looked into the little square mirror she had brought with her out of vanity, or out of spite for what she had left behind. She saw that her skin had tanned, her hair was greasy, her eyebrows weren't plucked, and she looked tired. Angry at the image, her face suddenly changed. For a second or two, she recognized a familiar expression—willpower. She knew those eyes; they belonged to the woman who had given birth to her: her mother's eyes in her face. They spoke of challenge, struggle, quest—but not defeat. For the first time, she drew breath from a past that joined the impassive reality of the day.

Rowing, walking, carrying, camping, eating, sleeping, breaking camp, rowing—that was her life. The life she had chosen now, that she had borrowed from her ancestors; an heiress by choice. The path had been broken by thousands of other travellers. All she had to do was follow them and believe in the promise of an easier day. She gathered the purity of water in her hands, free, with survival her only constraint. Surrounded by tall spruce and stunted deciduous trees, she saw rabbit tracks and spotted the silent partridge. She thanked the four other women for having helped her to persevere. She thanked the heavens for its sweetness on these May evenings. To her very last step, she thanked the Creator for having guided her.

◄▲►

The rain woke me that morning. Thousands of drops were
breaking on the blue waterproof canvas. The sky was grey.
The pine branches covered the ground like a carpet and sent
up their perfume. Walls of fabric formed a perfect triangle
above my head. The cool air was quickly warmed by the stove
set on bricks—just to be careful. I was awake, but I closed my
eyes so as not to miss any of this reality, this sense of being.
I breathed in the air, both warm and chilled, as deeply as I
could. I've been breathing it as far back as my people can
remember.

The tent is a makeshift shelter, a legacy, the choice of the
nomad, rest after a long hike, the most peaceful kind of sleep,
canvas stretched over wooden poles.

He who was beautiful. She who prayed that others might feel better. He who made drums from caribou hide, with his hands rough from stripping pine boughs and building roads. She who fed us freshly baked bread with melted butter and spaghetti with tomato and bacon sauce. He who moved to the new reserve when others refused. He who smoked; she who was at my prom, my graduation, during my child's first days. She who lived through the twentieth century without ever speaking a word in French but, in our language, always found the right word to name every modern thing and threat to her freedom. He whose children, all of them, were born in tents. He who never sold off his land. Those who once travelled the country, from ocean to ocean, never staying in the same place—and the people we have become since.

You were a hunter, a nomad, a survivor. You grew older, you stopped felling spruce, you bequeathed your struggles, and they were never lost.

The drum that's in the chest of drawers—you made it with your hands. You tanned the caribou hide, you chose the tree to cut down, and turned it into a firm wooden circle, the width of a big man's hand. Once the little bones that echo the drumbeat were attached to the cord, once the paint was dry and the circle perfect, you beat the drum three times with your fingertips. The sound was like a heart. The sound of a slow, sad heart echoed on the skin that was nearly white and as soft as a partridge's belly.

People from the city say we'll have to leave the bay. They talk long and hard. They want to move the reserve farther away, but still on the banks of the river. They'll build a school there, with houses and streets. Some listen to them, then walk away. The bay doesn't belong to those people; it's yours. You won't leave this plot of land: you'll stay for the challenge, out of love and pride. Standing on your two Indian feet, you resist, with fear in your belly but still courageous, with the ancient courage of the first people who tamed this country long ago.

You know the names of the rivers and the trees by heart. The mountains and the valleys, the plants that heal and the plants that harm. You can name the winds and the seasons, the wet snow and the blizzards. You know the animals and their young. But because there are so many, sometimes you forget the names of your grandchildren, and the children of your grandchildren.

You miss her every day, ever since she's been gone, the woman who gave you fourteen children. Who cooked the bread, who sewed the moccasins. You remember her when she was twenty, gathering pine branches to make a carpet under the tent. You remember her, as if no time had passed. You cry because you can't recognize her face and smell among the other faces that you know. She calls to you ceaselessly. They call this land *Nutshimit* with its lakes set among the mountains, rich with the things of the earth. When the wind rises, something inside you urges you to go. In your old grey pickup, with a grandson next to you, you drive along the 138, past the Mani-utenam gas station. Spruce and pine stand close on both sides of the road, pointing to the heavens. You turn onto a bumpy dirt road. A few tents are pitched on the banks of a river whose current is cold. This is the time of year when fishermen try to get the salmon to bite, in June, when the sun's warmth hasn't yet brought out the flies. You don't talk much, but your silence and sighs sound like boredom. Your grandson looks out the open window. Will he learn the path of tradition? It frightens you, like something inevitable. The way men have of leaving at the appointed time. The way your bones ache and, in your prayers to the Creator, you know the time is approaching. With a sudden stroke or in the slowness of disease, it will take you too, the big man with the grey hair, who has acquired the knowledge of an entire people, who has fathered numerous proud children.

You, *Anikashan*.

◄▲►

This is what comes back in memory: her short, greying hair. A
long flower-print dress cut from flimsy cotton and, on top of
it, an apron tied over the belly that carried nineteen children.
Her brown skin with freckles on her shoulders and arms, nose
and cheeks. A round face with small almond eyes. I thought
she was old, but no one else seemed to notice it. She was
always busy in her house, making bread, sewing moccasins,
embroidering flowers, stretching gut for snowshoes, asking
us, sometimes, to brush her hair. She breathed hard when
she held the needles between her tightly closed lips. She
didn't laugh when we lost the remote for her TV set. When
she wanted to rest, she would rock herself in her chair, but
always with a length of cloth in her hands so she could go on
working. We called her *Tshukuminu*, as if she were the grandmother of the whole world.

She wasn't like other grandmothers. She didn't let time slip
away. She didn't hurry off to do useless errands. She didn't
look after other people's kids to stave off boredom. She worked
at home, more artist than artisan. She fed her grandchildren
and was devoted to her husband. Pious, and not much for talk.
She was grand with the grandeur that comes with age. Serious,
almost severe, she took on her woman's role. Sometimes
she would laugh, and then she was beautiful, as if happiness
had finally caught up with her, and she couldn't avoid it any
more. My grandmother's laughter is forever written into my
childhood.

◂▲▶

At four o'clock, he wakes up. He cries because he's hungry.
He screams for his food. His mother hurries to warm the
milk. She hurries even though she knows he's not going to
starve to death. She tries to soothe him by rocking him in
her arms, gently and tenderly. She's been playing mother for
two months now. At night her sleep is fitful. Sometimes she
goes on rocking him, rocking and rocking. Her own mother
sleeps in the room next door. Her tears flow—from fatigue, of
course. This house hasn't been hers since she was seven. The
pink room isn't hers any more. Her child's body, her cheeks
swelling with laughter. She wants to be rocked too.

◂▴▸

The risk of not getting pregnant is greater than the other way around. All the girls want to give birth. As soon as they find someone willing, they stop using protection and wait for their bellies to swell. Shannon is afraid she'll never carry life inside her. In her despair, a sad child, she gets angry at her own mother, who conceived eight children effortlessly. She wants to be like all the other girls and have a baby in a stroller who will be hers, something for herself.

A child is a little ball of warmth, a dream, whether it's a boy or a girl, an ultrasound, a parcel of reality, a heart beating fast, wealth, a way of being loved, future profit, a way of existing, strengthening the nation that others want to decimate, lust for life, and the will to stop dying: a child.

When he's born, she won't even have her driver's licence yet, just her learner's permit. She'll blush when people ask her what her little brother's name is. She'll wait up alone till midnight on party nights, in a house not nearly spacious enough for her princess dreams. She'll be twenty on his fifth birthday.

When she's twice his age, she'll start thinking he's catching up to her. Young and beautiful—thirty years old is nothing. At sixteen, he'll be angry at her for not having been up to the task. He'll whimper like an animal for the new pair of shoes he'll never wear anyway. He'll transform what's missing into silence, and blame his silence on the youth, carelessness, and irresponsibility of his parents. He'll shout at her that he was an accident, and he won't be wrong.

But he'll have her eyes. His gurgling will sound sweet, and there will be splendour in his awkwardness. She'll burn with the desire to live as he nurses. When he's born.

◄▲►

She laughs and downs the cans of Bud they hand her. Stay, they tell her. She knows she won't go home tonight. Her mother will wait up, maybe she'll even go looking for her on the reserve. Why is her mother that way? Her friends can go home late or not go home at all. They get drunk every day, they take pills that make them ecstatic, they go from bed to bed. She'd like to be free with the kind of freedom she deserves because she's sixteen. But she's caught in a moral web. She'd like to be like them and wake up the next day with a hangover and a big fat hickey on her neck. Here, tonight, on the edge of the bay, behind the spruce and pine, sitting in front of a bonfire, contemplating it, no one will be able to find her.

◂▴▸

He started fishing very late in life. He was twenty when he
landed his first trout in a stream by Mile 60, near his grandfather's camp. That's where he bagged his first partridge too.
He must have been born for the hunt, but no one had known
that about him. His rabbit snares were perfect, and no animal
could avoid them. When he cast the fly, he knew the trout
couldn't resist.

Now he's forty. He was hired by the Band Council to
fish in the salmon river. There are two kinds of salmon: the
utshashumek[u] that swims to the sea then fights its way back
up the river. It's big and tastes of the salty ocean waves. And
there's the *pipunamu* that never leaves fresh water. It's smaller
and easier to catch. He fishes all day long in the middle of the
current, drifting, motor off. His skin turns brown as the fish
add up, the big ones and the little ones.

On the street that runs past the clinic, past the school and
the skating rink, you can always see those four kids following
behind Lise. She had them one right after the other. Now the
eldest, a boy, walks faster than she does. His three little sisters
giggle behind her back. They walk down Pashin Street on
their way to see *nimushum* and *nukum*. She has her babies,
but not her husband. He disappeared too soon, three years
ago. Too soon to hold his little girl, his youngest child. Too
soon—or too late in the night, and too drunk when he got on
the road to go to his house on Kamin Street. That house is full
of children's laughter, children who don't quite understand,
who forget too fast. The five of them walk past as if, on that
sunny afternoon, nothing bad could ever happen.

I wanted to bring you to a place where outsiders rarely set foot, where the train drops you with your bags, with just the essentials, at this deserted spot. It is hidden behind a spruce forest that, come winter, gives off the clear white sheen of a frozen lake, the same colour as your skin. I wanted you to see the forest, virgin to its very roots; I wanted you to hear the perfect silence of the wind at twilight. At night, we would have lain down on the thick carpet of snow, dressed like Eskimos, and admired the January aurora. Like two lovers. You would have cut the wood that would have kept us warm when evening came. I would have boiled the soup and cooked the bread just to hear you say, That warms the heart.

You saw the reserve, the overcrowded houses, the broken fences, the averted eyes. You said, With a little grass it would look okay. We slept in the house where I grew up.

But what I really wanted to share with you is that unspeakable pride of being me, entirely myself, without makeup or perfume, in that horizon of woods and whiteness. And the grandeur too, the kind that humbles even the mightiest on earth. Following the path of the caribou, you would have seen the tenacity of men faced with the cold, more alive than ever, finally living within their customs. Returning from the hunt, there would have been rabbit and bannock, and sweet tea to warm you. For a few days, you would have lived on the land of my ancestors, and you would have understood that grass doesn't naturally grow on sand.

◀▲▶

Everything fits into one room. The main wall faces the lake.
The right side of the room serves as a kitchen. Daylight comes
in through the window in front of the table. The upper cupboards are fashioned out of rough plank-ends and hold sugar,
coffee, jam, molasses, Carnation milk, mismatched cups,
plates big and small, colourful cereal for the kids' breakfasts,
brown sugar, oatmeal, soft butter in a dish, a box of stale cook-
ies, canned soup, pork and beans, corn, shortening, a con-
tainer of dried ground caribou meat, tea bags, and some small
packets of yeast, salt, and pepper. In the lower cupboards are a
few heavy pots that have outlived their usefulness at the house,
along with a sack of flour, a half-full bag of potatoes, the little
tub for doing the dishes, dish soap, and big green and little
white garbage bags. The utensils are stored in a closed metal
canister on the wooden counter. The oven runs on a genera-
tor. The kitchen part is separated from the washing part by a
blackened stove in the middle of the room. Wet things hang-
ing from hooks above the stove are trying to dry: mittens, wool
socks, felt boot inserts, moccasins, toques, scarves, dish towels,
washcloths, sometimes men's and children's clothing, if the
woman of the house has decided to do a quick but necessary
wash. There's no washing machine; you wait to get home
for that. On the hot cast iron of the stove sits a teapot, always
full no matter what time it is, comfort after a long winter's
walk. On the wall to the left is a round mirror and a big bowl
with a flower pattern set on a small chest. A few toothbrushes

in a glass that isn't used for drinking. The white pot on the floor is for urgent needs at night. The toilet is outside. Lined up against the back wall, three large beds complete the little wooden cabin's furnishings. The blankets are thick because of the cold January weather, and the stove that is never stoked much at night. Despite the insulation, the walls welcome in gusts of icy wind, and people cover up underneath the down quilts. The bedside table is stained with wax, cigarette ash, felt-pen scribblings, the dust of long absences, time. In the corner, pictures of the Holy Virgin and Jesus are pinned to the planks. A photo of a child sitting on an old woman's lap, and behind them, a stunted, mangy pine that stands in for a Christmas tree. Both are at an angle to the photographer, and their eyes look elsewhere.

The old cabin stands 254 miles north of Sept-Îles. The place is deserted and guarded by enormous spruce trees. Snow covers the lake, and the low sky is pierced by countless milky fires. Everything exists in its immediacy. Everything is contrary to common sense. Everything rests—the old souls and the families on vacation.

What he knows he learned from his grandfather. How to recognize the path the rabbit travelled and the bushes where the partridge shelters. The rifle pointed right at the spot where the caribou will appear two seconds later. How to survive for days on end, waiting for the herd, when ice forms on the lakes. What he knows he has been practicing since he stopped using drugs. He has made himself a new future.

Hundreds of them have crossed the line. Men have pitched tents, with a few women too. They were forbidden to cross the line, as if nature with its perfect laws had set down the borders of survival. Ecologists fear that the caribou, those nomadic herds that linger only to move on again, will go extinct. The Innu fear their own extinction. Despite the easy way that has been offered, they have never stopped venturing onto frozen lakes to bring back fresh meat for their families.

They let the animal rest for a night, to let it die, out of respect. The next day, the men cut up the legs, head, and ribs. They keep the hide for the artisans who will tan it. They will make bags, moccasins, and drums. The women take the large sides of meat that the men have brought them and cut them into smaller pieces. They put the bones aside, for they are precious. Later, they will boil them to extract the marrow and the fat. Once it is cooled, the grease spread on fresh bread will be the most coveted food of the feast. Several families' freezers will soon be filled with the meat of the *atik*^u.

He learned from his years as a hunter and discovered his

instinct. He says, without arrogance, like a promise: It's written in our blood. We'll find the caribou wherever he is.

He took the train this morning. On his back, he was carrying
his beige canvas bag stuffed with well-worn, warm clothing.
His two boxes full of canned goods, sugar, flour, and cigarettes
were already on the train, in the freight car. He was smoking
nervously as he prepared to board and leave his reserve for
three months. People around him were saying goodbye. Some
were leaving for the hunt, others to see family in Schefferville.
He was leaving to preserve his existence. He had put off this
trip for a long time, though he'd sworn up and down that he'd
do it, promising his friends who were drunker than he was.
Just last week, alone in his new house that was barely finished,
he had stopped believing. The endless nights, the illusions
on which you build your foundations. He put away cases and
cases of twenty-four, and the white powder stuck to the walls
of his weakened heart, its beating fading away as he laughed
one more time at life — its misunderstandings, its very incoher-
ence. That night, he swore out loud he would take the train
for *Nutshimit*.

NIKUSS

Go driving and find somewhere you want to stop out of respect for the sacred places, for the souls that have passed. I walk a few steps, then go around a metal fence put there to keep out others who might not respect this place. Grass grows, someone cuts it, it grows back again, fed by the stilled bodies of people, some of whom I know, a name or a face, or even a distant connection of blood that returns to memory. Some of them are strangers. I linger over those who seem familiar. The sound of the waves, the silence of a reserve, the few seconds it takes to calculate the years of someone's life, the age another one was when she passed. I notice a caribou carved into a brown stone that looks like bronze. Two short curving lines that stand for mountains; this is the work of hands accustomed to beauty. Plastic roses in a wicker basket stand next to a bouquet of real yellow flowers that have hardly faded at all.

It's not easy to try to understand the life of a person you've never met. In your fruitless attempt, you hit a wall so violently you lose all understanding. Better stand back from the carved stone if you don't want to crush the man underneath. You recognize yourself in the name, but you don't know where it comes from or anything about his existence. You regret coming here: an unknown woman on dead ground. You'd be better off leaving.

There is an ancient belief among the Innu: They say that if a father never saw his child, that child has a gift.

It's a house like all the others, with green walls and brown beams. The stairs are in good shape, just a few cracks in the wood that speak of time passing. They are as old as I am. My very first steps are written there, as are all the others I leave every time I visit. My footsteps fit me perfectly, small marks on a white background that describe the life of a child to the age of seven. The room was ideal for three little girls, and another room next to it for an older brother who didn't like their fighting.

Behind the house lies a little forest as small as we once were. There were raspberries and blueberries, just what we needed on those hot July days. The spruce trees were stunted, but they stood up to the wood planks my brother nailed into them to make a barricade. Today, a clinic and a convenience store take their place. The fence that separates the house from the parking lot doesn't stop the drunks—or anyone else.

My mother is trying to get grass to grow on the sand, and I congratulate her every time I see a bunch of clover sending out its leaves. The windows, floors, and paint should be redone. The house has aged, the way I have, I suppose. Things age faster back there, where I come from. Sometimes people don't even see it.

‹▲›

I lower the lights in the living room. Baby sleeps and won't
wake till it's time to drink, then he'll fall asleep again at my
side in this bed too big for my solitude. I sit down on the love-
seat I bought at the flea market for a third of what it's worth.
It's red, like the autumn painting I got when I turned twenty,
like the feather pillow that invites me to laze on the sofa, like
the back of my little boy's hobbyhorse.

◂▲▸

Tonight, I don't know why, I feel like the world is falling away behind me. Maybe that's not the right way to put it. Nothing confuses me more than the clear salty liquid that runs from my puffy eyes onto my cheeks. I've never wanted to be some-one else the way I do now, an immigrant from a far-off land, come to lose herself here. My body isn't mine any more. My pounding heart keeps reminding me of that. I pull away from what I have always been, from what I always thought I repre-sented. I try not to make noise, and my sobbing fades to the rhythm of my steps on the floating floor. Water can't slake a third of my thirst, and I feel myself drifting to a stop, the way cars do at a red light. I never sang before, so why would I start now?

The snow has frosted over the windows of my apartment. Soon condensation will form from the boiling soup that warms the scent of my emptiness. Between what stays outside and what comes through the door, between those who go past my door and those who come in and sit at my table, the door stands straight with no fear of being forced. That door is the only way in and out, and I am the woman of the house. That's not much, but it gives me a feeling of great power, as if I were invulnerable. I realize that some people who leave here might never come back, but I let them go and smile as I tell them goodbye. Solitude weighs heavily on my heart; I turn it into a source of vanity. It lies lightly on my pain, the way snow covers the streets around my house. But I always let the men go when they make a move for their coats.

I don't have the luxury.

Collapse leads to a vegetative existence, and vegetables, as everyone knows, are good only for feeding people. No right to collapse tonight, despite the fatigue and tears that keep me up, half-asleep, in post-partum exhaustion.

I don't have the choice because I don't have the luxury. Men study and reflect on the superhuman elements of existence. They set down frameworks for themselves, they lead examined lives, and they forget what's essential.

That's not a platitude, it's the simple truth: I don't have the luxury to let my mind get lost in a cloying, insensitive labyrinth. All that matters is what can be served up on a piece of bread.

Of course I should never forget my nomad's instincts, ceaselessly searching for a state of grace.

But leaving is impossible for me now. I would need time, and I don't have it, any more than I have the luxury, like the beauty of an old painting, like traces of time caught in the frame of a cave. Girlhood dreams fade when it's time to nurse.

Artists have brushes, all the brushes they need. My only artwork is a red-and-yellow gouache on a giant sheet of white paper that will decorate a baby's apple-green bedroom.

I opened the book with the beige cover and the gilt binding. On the glossy paper is the young gaze of a dark-eyed face. It forgot to smile, and the cheeks, red with heat, were unmoving. The lines around the eyes were shut tight. The mouth was doubting and cared nothing for the image that would result. But that young skin—it will keep its grain and its beauty as long as I live.

◂▲▸

A teenage girl is grateful when a man she doesn't know tells her, You have his eyes, the same wide, dark eyes as your father.

He is like his grandfather: an Innu's brown skin. She keeps saying the words, *Uinipapeushu Nikuss*. Babies are paler these days. But he's a real Indian, you can tell.

‹▲›

You will draw a tree with your fingers in the delicate sand of the bay. Your only company will be the waves rolling in. Infinity stands before you, with the water that follows the current up to the blue of the sky, the slack water of a hot July day. You'll see the places I used to swim when I was little. I will tell you that even the earth can be deformed by human grasping, the water sullied by contempt for everything that does not bring riches. Your childhood will bring comfort to the seven-year-old I was. Your fresh eyes will see the beauty of the world for the first time. Your laughter will be the echo of my hopes. The sun will set as we look on, our thoughts elsewhere. No mist, no rain, no weighty past to stifle the living. Silence will envelope our dreams of the future. By the shore and the tides we will stand, *Nikuss*.

NAOMI FONTAINE, a member of the Innu First Nation, was born in Uashat, Quebec, a community with a population of less than 5,000. She was an education student when she wrote *Kuessipan*, her first novel, which she based on her own experience. She lives in Quebec City

DAVID HOMEL, born and raised in Chicago, is a two-time Governor General Literary Award-winning translator and writer. Among his numerous translations are the works of Dany Laferrière, including *How to Make Love to a Negro* and *The World is Moving around Me: A Memoir of the Haiti Earthquake*; his own novels include *Sonya & Jack, Electrical Storms, The Learning Curve*, and *Midway*. He lives in Montreal.